School Dad

Poetry Blog: www.amazulugaming.com
Instagram: Onepoeticgamer
Twitch: www.twitch.tv/onepoeticgamer

ISBN 978-0-578-83657-7

Published by
AmaZulu Gaming, LLC

Cover, Logo and Illustrations done by
Christopher James Rowland

contact info for CJ Rowland
Instagram - **istimyouleye**

Final Edition
Printed in the United States of America

Table of Contents

Period 1

Period 2

Lunch Time

Period 3

Period 4

ISS

Homeroom

Preface

If you are looking for nice and neat, this book is nothing of what you are expecting. If you are easily offended, you can put the book down now, as this is poetry from "MY" last 16 years in education.

School Dad reflects my thoughts from experiencing you and your children. I use to think a dad should be particular things, but now, I'll just be what's needed for those that look to me to be a "dad". I have so much respect to all the fathers that continue to be in their children's lives. Thank you to all the parents that allowed me the opportunity to be a part of your child's life and have welcomed me into your family.

Period 1

The Intro (2005)

This be the intro
and you know what time it is
when the school bell rings
I'm a superhero to kids
and for today's subject
we must politic this and that
to be more specific
poetic tracks that sound like raps
whether you're white or black
tan, brown, yellow or red
before you leave here
you'll be quoting something I said
with no regrets
for what I'm putting in your head
it's the positive energy
that won't have you mislead
and I'm far from finished
even though soon you'll clap hands
but true props go to your teachers
so make sure you listen
to the things that they're saying
so you won't end up missin'
the opportunity of a lifetime
it's your education that you're grippin'
don't get caught slippin', trippin'
thinking you pimpin'
if you can't read or write
then you forgo the mission
can't add, subtract or multiple

then it's you causing the division
basic math facts you need to succeed
so please pay attention
is there something I'm forgettin'
oh yeah, I almost forgot
on this poetic journey
my name is Mr. B-Dot
and I've decided to stop
to kick it with all of you
so let's get this thing going
with no further ado
it's my intro and you know
what time it is
as I finish this one off
the poetic journey begins.

Hey Mr. Williams, I don't know
if you remember me. But i'm a
senior now, I was in 5th grade
at Wakelon in 2007 and was in
the poetey club; just wanna
show you how far i've come
since then. https://
m.youtube.com/watch?

Let Me Hear You Say YES
(Elementary Dreams)

We going to Disney World
let me hear you say YES
recess before lunch
let me hear you say YES
4's on the EOG
let me hear you say YES
but it's ok to make 3's
let me hear you say YES
schools out because of snow
let me hear you say YES
a field trip to the zoo
let me hear you say YES
I got a visitor for lunch
let me hear you say YES
I won student of the week
let me hear you say YES
a party on Friday
let me hear you say YES
a group project with my friends
let me hear you say YES
a sleep over this weekend
let me hear you say YES
my team won the last game
let me hear you say YES
we earned a concert for free
let me hear you say YES
this is about him, hear and me
let me hear you say YES
let me hear you say YES
let me hear you -say- YES!

The Playground

On the grounds where we play
you might find on bright days
the kids who parlay in parks all day
bring kick balls, jump ropes
hola hoops my way
then say what I say
red or green light,
and I hope it doesn't get cloudy
because we have to watch when rainy
wishing blue skies would stay
would like to play all day
on the playground,
got these kiddies on a mission
that stay racin' cause they winning
hope those slow one's listen
fixing to get with it
freeze tag cause she did it
dodge ball get him hit
better duck or get licked
be on the sideline throwing fits
here's the pitch off the switch
better come with the full swing
for what they bring makes people fling
on strike three hear everybody sing
on the playground,
as they move right to left on stealth
hide and seek for the health
exercise like its wealth
despite how they're chillin' with self,
on the playground.

Heeey

I make the boy say heeey
the girl say heeey
this is how the kids respond when
they in the third grade
Gordan say heeey
Jocelyn say heeey
they making noise to signify it's not ok
I tapped Savannah on the shoulder
she wasn't ready for the play
she looked right, I moved left
then all of a sudden came a heeey
Tyler G couldn't see why I was yelling out nay
UNC is not for me because I go for NC State
McCants, Felton, Williams even down to Sean May
say goodbye to UNC, it's NBA, he said heeey
I make the boy say heeey
the girl say heeey
this how the kids respond when
they in the third grade
Darius say heeey
Eliza say heeey
they making noise to signify it's not ok
the girl Markie, the boy Jennings
Alex T and D and Ramsey
Holly, Katie and Ashley
they keep on asking, I keep on laughing
while they napping, I get to clapping
wake'em up all while I'm passing
looking dazed, like hey what happen

I make the girl say heeey
the boy say heeey
this is how the kids respond when
they in the third grade
Latay say heeey
Alexis say heeey
they making noise to signify it's not ok!

Elementary Monday Morning

Early morning sunshine with young minds
collaborating to learn,
spirits on high, talkative
but not with negative intent
getting directed to stay focused
as there's a goal in mind
even though they may not peep it,
see, they're daydreaming about recess
lunch and after school politics
yet, let's flip the switch
so we can light up souls
because,
we're here for education
and a hidden agenda to
restore hope,
as I sit observing innocence
wishing,
it could always stay that way.

Period 2

Young Black Boy
(You are not a color)

Young black boy
I see you smiling
young black boy
I see you climbing
they can't stop you, here's your confidence
I will not drop you when the others have left.
Young black boy
I see you hurting
young black boy
no need for cursing
failure comes when you take their ways
follow truth and you'll prolong your days.
Young black boy
it's me you copy
young black boy
no one can stop the
role model I have to be
because in me I see you now believe.
Young black boy
I see you smiling
young black boy
I see you climbing
they can't stop you, please remember these words
success will come just use all you've learned
young black boy
I feel you smiling
young black boy
I hear you climbing

young black boy
I see you laughing.
young black boy
I know you're passing
young black boy…

Baby Girl

Looking back on the first day
you walked in class
a reflection of frustration could be felt from
your aura,
wondering how at the age of seven
could your life be filled with such heavy baggage
might be the lack of spiritual love
mentally being shoved in the face with hate
and no father to help erase
or relate such pain
no place to rest comfortably
despite your surroundings being filled by a family
broken,
would it even matter if
I could hand you peace in pieces
hold this ray of sunshine
to your eyes from mine
align our current timeline
so we'd have this father daughter connection
a blessing, that feels like a good dream
but you wake up to a curse
that has me watching you live a misconception
of family dynamics that
ride you home to address sorrow
questions that end in why
while being gifted empty promises
left with the short end of the stick
with the expectation of getting by
like everyone else

band aids don't help to heal self
as I'm watching peripherally
cause when I do so directly
you react explosively to the pain
the shame that can be changed
as I extend a helping hand
in hopes you don't turn away
if not today, maybe tomorrow
baby girl.

In His Soul

Locked down in the depths of his soul
only he knows why he's acting this way
why he explodes daily
shuts down on "them" completely
then can't look at me
barely speaks
after he just finished yelling at "them"
yes "them"
don't take "them" as a color
because it's some other demon he's fighting
trying to stay alive
and die at the same time
you not gonna understand why
because even he can't
and I'm the in-between
trying to put it in words
have it make sense
add it to some logic
and subtract the bullshit you keep getting
wondering what is missing
and we'll start at
a father, a hero and the truth
so "they" call in
psychiatrists, counselors and religion
hoping to find the fix
but none of that is "it"
none of that mixes like oil and water

even when it's holy
and these holes he can't fill
spitting as he curses
words learned from dem boyz
crooked lies he creates
to flow through straight teeth
got tired of beef
so he started cooking up his own ideas
his own plots, schemes and dreams
but now the water's hot
at the boiling point
and he's lost his directions
meanwhile, in his midsection
his gut telling him to make the right move
but-he-don't-know-what-to-do
and as his mentor, his mirror look-a-like
his one way ticket he doesn't even know he has
I've been given the task of saving his life
or possibly
prolonging his death
either way it would seem
the world is on our shoulders
and the colder it gets
the more I recognize
the answer doesn't reside with this heat
it just keeps running with the wind that was gone
when there was time to write novels
about American boys that descended from Africa
that had a chance even when
the deck was stacked in
someone else's favor.

Fork at the Road

Now that they label me the hero
where do I go at the crossroads
as this life is about decisions
and just because there is hope that they'll succeed
doesn't mean someone like me will step in
when he gets to stressin'
wondering, have I given him the tools
to compensate
or, was I the one that makes the difference
ever since my inception
I kept the powers that be
second guessing on deployed life lessons
or were they confessions
arming little ones with mental secret weapons
that I just so happen to be supplying them with
so you can guess the possible outcome
if I left, because when I'm gone
the hidden rules I'm trying to teach
might not be reached
common sense you'd think
wouldn't be passed on
double meanings are like the standards they face
and the blues aren't just sad songs
but why ask
if little ones aren't learning the task
it won't stop the pressure from coming fast
at this fork in the road
on the verge to explode
cause they don't know about my debt load

middle class living
poverty pay checks me into a hold
so I'm sold on being a survivalist
having to chase cream with only one chance
despite a lifetime dream to fulfill my passion
or so it seems
these little one's have missing needs
so what will they believe if I leave
damn it, I know we both can achieve
we're like...are family
so my role he models is what frees
him from focusing on bad choices
thinking his only way out is sports
and, which way am I pressing to
with this pressure at the fork
I'm labeled as a hero
but if I'm not here to support
what is going to become
of those that now need me?

I Watch My Future

I watched my future die today
in drops of rain from my eyes
and nobody realized it
but me,
knowing I could do no more than watch
in a FUBAR system
I must acknowledge I am a part of,
there is no love and little hope
for me to be superman
to save the day
because for every second I make a save
another kid gets slayed
another path is paved in a statistic book
because I lost him to suspension, a gang
a broken home, a music video with video hoes
and what am I suppose to tell him
when he's promised the world for his soul
when it's shown there's no control
and the only stock
is in a jump shot, an unfair catch
taking a gun and pressing it to the neck
of the same one who's teaching him to respect
they need so much more
and I can only offer them less
as I must confess that it's not logical
for an 8-year-old who can't recognize his ignorance
after he just got suspended,
when he's thinking and then telling me
"Mr. Williams, I'll be back next week

so it don't really matter to me"
see, he has already been retained
and not because he wasn't smart enough
to pass the grade
it's because he missed too many days
so what am I suppose to say
that, it's going to be ok
and what are you going to tell me
"Billy, I didn't know it was this way,"
WAKE UP PEOPLE
can't you see that we're dying
don't you know that it's more than one person lying
and this was me trying' to explain this frustration
but I'm caught up in hesitation
meditating as,
I watched - my future - die today
and no, you can't tell me I'll be ok
so please hold your applause
I won't be needing it
because tomorrow, this kid
will still be needing this
love, they say I cannot give
this role, he is taught not to model
the truth can be hard to swallow
so I'm left to choke and die
which, upon further thought
may be better than having to live
with a future and a hope
that's a lie.

Lottery

He waited on a round ball
spun in a hollow sphere
that felt like slow motion
only it wasn't for a sports team draft pick
no, he waited on coincidence
destiny and fate,
for his number
which while freshly assigned to him
the system has always socially secured him
as a number,
so as the balances begin to weigh out
with choice having as much of a chance
as justice dealt by a blind folded lady
he waited for his number to be called
for the possibility of an education
at the best school
with the best teachers
and whatever word you desire
to put behind best
except that,
best doesn't describe the situation he faces
if his number doesn't get called...

Inside the Room

I use to watch the shadows dance
under door cracks
hearing voices crack
high pitched screams
and the sounds of destruction coming from
inside the room
booms that made buildings falling
seem like ant piles blowing in the wind
moans saying "no"
voices yelling
hoe - shit - damn
-Bitch-
I can't understand this
clutch this G.I. Joe has
wishing I could be the superhero
that saves the day
make the screams go away
but here in the shade of the couch
my soul witnesses the eternal heartbreak
that leaves me with the shakes at night
sweating pools of tears
that won't reduce the fears
the pain between my ears
as I nightmare for normality
by any means
even if it minuses me
as the rage tormented me
for a decade

and this love
it turns to hate
and I can't win an Oscar
because I can't fake this
and I can only watch
the shadows dance and wish,
they were only dancing
for something besides
me.

This Is How A Killer Starts

You call him gay
or he's a fag
won't except him cause he has no cash
his uncle molest him
when he's alone
and so did his pastor
so who's left at home
to protect the necks of an innocent prospect
the check is less
than that of which
paid to free slaves
building up this kids rage
and hating his race
then thinking he doesn't save
that energy, clouded memories
expecting the best
from a mom and dad
that's under the influence
now he's mad, this lad
in which you still call fag
because he reads books
and girls just went past
as you laughed, yeah you mashed
his hopes as on him you gagged
couldn't even be courteous
in this line, he goes last
whispered secrets about his sister
said the girl was too fast
and openly voted he

would be the most likely to go drag
and you had your chance to save him
but kept love when he passed
claiming to never understand
the reasons he was mad
it was sad, you were glad
when the newspaper showed how he was bad
reported all his business
yet they still missed the true facts
of how you contributed
to a flame that you help spark
and you wondered what it was
that helped make this killer start.

See This Right Here

See this right here
begins where a life ends
when he couldn't take his last breath
because so called death caught it
and nobody seems to be paying attention,
not even Superman can save him
cause time has ticked its last tock
and an angel said it was time to go
it didn't matter who's side he was on
or what spot he represented
north, west, south, east
peace came at last but what kind of peace is that
where life is full of contradiction
and there is no winning
but I'm glad he got it
because I still don't have the answer
this ain't no cancer or even some rare disease
so please stop waiting around for the punch line
the bottom line has become the drum line
and I'm drawing a line
where I've dared you to cross it
but since my influence can't cover that cost
and I'm not paid out the behind
sporting good looks that some would consider fine
I find that this thin line between love and hate
has turned into a big brick wall
and it's standing between me and ya'll
see this one right here

came a little too late
skip the after thought before the date
there won't be any shaking this young man up
because he's broken down
and no sounds are coming from his mouth
not even shallow breaths
can't get a faint heart beat
his sweat still fresh from five minutes ago
on the playground playing football
he was living his sports dream
but now, that's all it's ever gonna be
we, can't bridge the gap or fill in this hole
because this hell I'm now facin'
got me questioning God even if it ain't right
for nothing won't be replacing
eleven years, eight days away from twelve
and can you tell me what I should think
at 28 when I should be making babies,
but, I'm burying one who danced like an angel
nickname my heartbreak troubled
cause see this right here
is serious and nobody was hearing this
four months ago when
I spoke about my love for Baby Girl
seeing my Future Dy-ing
and now… now
a little boy lies dead
and my tears won't bring him back
none of my cursing can relax
my soul now on pause
ready to die cause he no longer lives
and, I know you ain't feeling me

and this pressure is killing me
so this got's to be what Christ felt
when he screamed
"God, why have you forsaken me?!"
cause you took James and Baby Girl got raped
now I got this gauge, a .45 and whole lot of hate
that I wished was replaced with the love that was
taking from me
cause they took-a part-of Billy
and I tried to take it easy
but No-Bo-Dy was hearing me
so now, Some-Bo-Dy should be fearing me
cause I have had it
not up to here but way up there
and I no longer care if rhyme has a reason
as it's a new season
and I'm feeling so all alone
forget this king's throne
because when I had the whole world
in the palm of my hands
I couldn't hold his
while his life was in my arms on the pavement,
children all around me thought I was omnipotent
but now…now
the buzzer sounded and I didn't even shoot
didn't choke but held him close enough
to feel his life cease
could probably see me desist
as his body departed from spirt,
you want to hug my heart
go look for it
Six-Feet-Deep

cause it rests in peace with two folded hands
that won't move again
eyes gazing into skies where he will rise
as I'm asking for a bit of peace while still alive
because this right here
this poem right here
is meant for him
but he's gone
and I feel like I was wrong
as I try to stay holding on
but I'm not that strong,
I am, not that strong
for even God died
so maybe, maybe so have I
so there is no understanding
ain't no need in me asking
because I don't have the words,
and despite how I try
my grace has been kicked to the curb
and you may have heard my soul morn
when it got torn
almost resulting to anything
to get my mind off the pain
because I can't perform
this next step, the next phase
and my thoughts have been running for days
with no water, no sustenance
so please forgive me if my words end on this page
because I've run out of things to say
and I still can't explain why…
why….
why?

You Have No Idea
(School System Blues)

You have no idea
what it is like
to be Superman.
X-ray my heart
see up into my soul
find the lives of little ones
God told me to hold
told me to mold
and treat as if my own
Black, White, Mixed
unify this until it's shown
a race that's one, called human
but less than that we're treated
I won't pretend
because while you sleep
I can hear the cries
I catch the tears falling from their eyes
I see the pains
I feel the gain
of increased pressure that
drives grown men insane
and they think it's a game to be played
life is unordinary in these school days
because now I'm dealing with
a boy with A.I.D.S.
now I'm dealing with
a six-year-old getting raped
now I'm dealing with
his momma dying
what do you tell a baby

when you feel like cryin'
as a man comes home and lays two hands
on their momma's face, please understand
these gangs got their guns to young deuces head
all of this while you've tucked your kids into bed
and it is said
it's heavy the crown on the king's head
these thorns are attached, these days that I dread
when I go get the young boy
to take him to the office
cause the counselor has to tell him
that inside a coffin
resides big brother who just OD'd
what are you trying to tell me
Superman takes bullets and
I got six buried inside me
cause they shot up her uncle
for his chain and money
and the young boys think
that it's cool to be a dummy,
so I want to thank ya
for believing the hype that you
drinking with rummy
currently I'm surrounded by kids of all colors
they calling me daddy because there is no father
soul brother that's like no other
I'm take'em all in
cause Superman don't care about color
why bother, I wonder what's fair and
because the world ain't caring
a man goes and molest a kid
and everybody start stare-in
dare-in me to make a mistake
another kid filled with hate

threatens to erase me if I don't get out of his face
come to my place, my space
and take these shots
they think Superman can't be hurt
but Superman can be dropped
and it's from thrown rocks
sticks and stones don't break bones
it's the knife in your back from
policies that lay prone
in position to get'em
into a form of submission
being Black ain't easy
try it against a whole system
where you're the only face that young ones see
that happens to be a male in the school society
at elementary, everybody be watching you
three fourths of the kids sitting back
want to be what you do
but adults question you
how you dress and who you be
question if you fit in with the other faculty
Clark Kent your way in to blend in with the trend
knowing they will soon call on Superman again
and the world you're caught in
is never too easy
come see for yourself if you don.t believe me
you'll see he, Superman
fighting for peace
you'll see he, Superman
"fighting" for "peace"
you'll see he, Superman
FIGHTING

FOR
PEACE,
and you have no idea
what it's like
to be Superman,
no- i-dea....

Because I Failed

Could you get up
if you never fell down
appreciate being on high
after coming from underground
the rocks are at the bottom
so I know my foundation is sound
heavy can be the head
not just when wearing the crown,
I mound all the losses
so when I'm high on success
I can see where I come from
and never forget
if it wasn't for being beaten
defeated temporarily
then winning is only something
I would consider a rarity
I barely or momentarily
feel bad when I fail
until I remember how well I'm now prepared
to lose nothing when there's
everything to gain
victory wouldn't taste so good
if I never knew pain.

Lunch Time

Freestyle VII

If E=MC squared
then poetry equals B dash Dot
down to the socks
so athletic
I got a foot and a half
of metaphors between my toes
Lamisil can't stop me
I whooped tough actin' Tinactin in less than 4 weeks
so I keep runnin' them
runnin'em into the dirt
cause I like'em dirty
except my free verse cause I don't curse
well, at least not in front of the kids
because ignorance seems to be the true trigger
and you figure I would drop such words
out of my poetic vocabulary
but most times words stink
like dodo and who knew
I'd have 4th graders trying to bust flows just like me
spit dialect off the spelling words we heard
now we hype when Akeelah
comes around for the bee
cause then we won't just be yelling out letters
to words we would have never used
we'll have the judges confused,
after we ask to have spelling words defined
through poetry
and of course he or she will try their best

to say we breakin' all the rules
but that's-what poets-do
so in the mean time
while others are slamming poetry to bias referees
I grab my balls
not cause I'm derogatory
but because I'm going bowling
cause what I'm holding can't be measured
by dysfunctional crowds
it has to be done aloud
while silent in a freestyle
written for the purpose of sparking the cypher
so while this internet microphone
still has battery power
let me ask you
who's next to decipher
Common said he use to love her
and now I like her
so what will this mean
when we meet in the middle of the ring
with rings
asking her if we can be the future king
I guess that remains to be seen
if I taste kind of funny
it's because I'm the black jellybean
and I have a dream
that one day
every poet will hold hands
but, until then
I'll pass the mic so someone else can come
and take a stand.

T.P.C. is The Poetry Club
"Poets in the making"

Meeting Place: Room 2508
Meeting Time: TBD

The Poetry Club
@ Heritage High

Do you like spoken word?

Interested in writing or
reading poetry???

Contact
Mr. Williams for
More Information
Room 2508

T.P.C.

The Poetry Club
Year 3
@ Wakelon Elementary

Friday's in the Media Center
12:35 PM - 1:10 PM
*extended time optional

Express Yourself!!!

T.P.C. is

"Poets in the making"

Are you in 5th Grade?

Interested in writing or
reading poetry???

Sign-Up sheet
In the
Media Center

Freestyle XIII

Ding, ding
the school bell rings
or is that the ring that starts the boxing match
see, they thought I shouldn't be here
should of left before the going got rough
before school shooters came through
with uzis and 9mms
figuring they'd show their artistic skills in blood
playing silence of the lambs
not knowing I'm the shepherd of this flock
cause I'm no longer the back up
no longer sitting on the bench warming up your spot
cause now I'm Tony Romo throwing T.O. the TDs
and then getting fined every week
for doing it my way
cause what I say has them off rhythm
as we be speaking in Black English Vernacular
just to mess wit'em
just so they can talk about our diction
but now you got's to mention
dem Black boys and girls sitting in Z-town
pulling 3 stars out the sky
and putting them on their report cards
we on the yard of the school of hard knocks
and we K.O.ing every hater
every racist, every sucka M.C.
with a B.A. saying they can teach
cause it goes beyond degrees

into the six separations of life
love, faith and understanding
if you ain't caring
we not pairing you up with our success
you can throw your best game at us
and we crossing over BS, dirt and lies
and making you fade away like a jump shot
so when the buzzing sound comes on
it's not from cell block D1 being closed
it's because you just received your third whammy
and this little devil is
whacking yo ass across the screen
and I don't mean to be doing you this kind of harm
but the alarmed started ringing
and you didn't stop the clock
cause by my watch I just turned thirty
and at 9:30
I got thirty of those same kids you talking shit about
giving me a standing ovation cause
God put me here
and right now I would swear out loud,
but the kids might be listening
so let me censor this and state that
any Micky Ficky trying to see me
has to deal with 600 plus babies
that come equipped with
loud mouths, smartasses
and energy that could out last the sun
so if you want to run with it
roll the dice
and when you pay that price

of getting beat into submission
you'll be wishing you had listened
when I freestyled about the kids I live for
that at moment's notice
will knock down your door
just cause I said it
and I bet if you think I'm pulling your leg
sit down in this wheelchair
and let me push you instead
cause the nation we building
isn't anywhere near
the contemplation you was thinking
I smell somebody's bum burning
cause this is cooking you up like ya bacon
and you won't be replacing these souls I touch
despite the vegetation they keep placing
between your ears
I'll be here for years
if it means these kids make it
you can call that dedication
which is impossible for me to fake
as it's a necessity
since no one was expecting me
I brought my own plate
so when I crash the party
and get naughty cause you didn't invite me
I didn't need no reservation from you flakes,
cause we making "super" out of stars
that the world has cast away
so consider this round our victory
next round what will you have to say?

Period 3

It Takes More Than Me
(apparently for some of these so called parents)

If God blesses the child
who has their own
then I suppose those children
not rich enough to buy in
are left to snatch crumbs at school tables
dreaming of a better day to come.
I use to think I could make a difference
but I found that when your kids call me daddy
because you're too busy to play
or even take the time to say
son, what are you thinking or
daughter, don't play games like that
it's not appropriate,
that you, the parent
(if I should even call you such)
have about as much love in you as the word shit
and as much directions as Nascar drivers
who can't remember
-turn left-
so, what good is my two cents I've given your child
if upon the time I send the child home
you are past the word tipsy and near blackout,
all this time I'm diggin' in their case asking
where's your homework
where's your homework
only for it to be found on the floor
as a means of catching your throw up
I've done some silly things before
but before I keep giving your kid an option
I'm going to make them write

I WILL NEVER TALK DURING CLASS TIME
AGAIN MR. WILLIAMS
as oppose to the
"don't do that again please, ok?"
because the only child trauma I needed
was the "thought" of getting my butt beat
to keep me in line
but now, it's a set up
to where grown people are controlled by children
and I can't tell who's the kid any more,
here I am thinking I'm doing too much
when really
mom and dad have their hands and head
up their bottoms
then come wanting to shake my hand,
the set up goes beyond politics and critics
or principals and superintendents,
it lays in the arms of the parents
who falsely give it to the teachers
expecting perfection, a happy meal
with a coke and a smile from me
saying in their minds,
"touch my kid and I'll sue you dummy"
or even
"I think my child is not getting what
he needs in school"
when really,
is the kid going home to a home,
because it's not me teaching them to say
"You Not My Damn Parent"
unbeknownst to the child

I will be temporarily if they say that again,
skip this job
it's not a future I'm concerned about,
it's when your then 18-year-old
who better say the right words
to my momma at the store
cause then,
it will be legal to whoop "they ass"
I'm not trying to be bad ass or sarcastic
what I am being is what you seemingly don't grasp
-responsible-
for what one day will be
our future.

Choices

Drunk guy sitting on the curb
he got choices
young boy standing on the corner
he got choices
old man trying to get a job
he got choices
everybody got their own choices
so what's yours?

-10 -
seconds sitting on the clock
balls in your court
what'cha you goin' do?
On one side you have
big dreams, future aspirations
and the hope for a better life where you're the star
-but-
sitting in your way
lies peer pressure
in the form of drugs, guns and red rum
with gangsters, so called killers
and your local pusher man
selling you a dream
-9-
but that dream can be a nightmare
and you may say that you never scared
but nobody cares
except those who love you
those who stand for your

guiding you on your way
-8-
so in order to get to your dream
you have to battle through a maze called life
where some things aren't fair
and the world doesn't revolve around you
so, it's time to press your luck
-7-
steady now, cause time is ticking
and it seems everybody is calling your name
do this, do that, go there, come here
so much movement you don't know
which way is up
and now it seems that everything is confusing
because for some reason
you can't see straight
-6-
but luckily, you have friends who hold you down
with the addition of positive influences
speaking good things like
you're the best, you da man, you're the one,
can I be down
can you show me how you do that
and before you know it
-5-
you feel like the king
but, heavy is the head that wears the crown
and what you gon' do
when those friends ain't around
left to self
trying to think, trying to contemplate
yet despite your haste

-4-
you're left with 20 questions that sound like
what's my next move, will I fail
is this really something I want to do
and who is coming with me
but evidently
-3-
you can't seem to see through the fog
and your path doesn't seem so clear now
and you'll do almost anything to get out of here
cause there's
-2-
seconds left
and your panicking, you got decisions to make
and they don't accept late work
cause here
it's either Do or Die
and in the sweet by and by
your wishing you had more time
cause you're
-1-
second away
from payday or rock bottom
they ask who's got the props
and you say I got'em
but in your moment of glory
a man comes to you
cause your time is up
and he has your fate in his hands
-and-
he points directly at you and asks
what - are you going - to do?

Drunk guy sitting on the curb
he got choices
young boy standing on the corner
he got choices
old man trying to get a job
he got choices
everybody got their own choices
so what's yours?

Because I Care

I will never be on a savior level
but if I don't make it happen
this little boy fails
that one that's in Kindergarten
while his daddy is in jail,
and the only thing that looks like
his father figure here
is me,
on average
when is the last time you've seen
three Black men working in an elementary school,
I can tell you're not ready for this hell
daily, of walking this path on Earth
looking at this young boy
showing his ass while at school
and think he's cool when I appear
instincts should tell him respectfully fear
but he already don't care,
talking to himself
cause nobody is there to listen
except the few dudes with attitudes
that hang out on the block,
rules mean nothing when the home is broke
and with what he's seeing
it can't be fixed with singing days of the week
especially with your stomach grumbling
teacher yelling out in the hallway
"follow the green box line on the floor"
and for some reason it's almost like

he's his daddy already
following a yellow line in the yard
one behind the other
and no, I'm not convinced
the tid bits I'm describing aren't enough of a hint
trying to live with myself knowing
these Black boys in front of me
don't know where they're going
not listening to positivity
cause at night, it don't tuck them into bed
kiss them on the head and ensure
that life is worth living,
so no matter how many times I keep saying
"you got to focus"
his focus is on making people laugh
to escape his pain
but when you're a grade behind
what's the purpose,
cause in the long run
the majority of people
that have the power to make a decision
will have him embracing Special Ed
this can't be just an imbalance in his head
he got potential that can't be enhanced
without his mental
so I pause and then wonder why
only 60 some odd years ago
Brown vs. Board of Education help make it so he
even has the option to learn
equally..lawfully…
depending on your point of view

but now, he saying he don't want to go to class
and I'm like, is there a choice
do I even need to ask
I'm going past sorry ass teachers
as excuses
and blaming the parents unveils only
half of the truth
as there is an inherited responsibility amongst us all
to piece together our future,
so just like it takes more
than one piece to make a bomb
it's everybody's job to prevent strong arm Rob
from using deadly weapons placed in his palms
but here I am 8 years prior
trying to explain to this kid's mom
that your son could be passing every grade
but if his behavior is off the page
by throwing fits and desks in a rage
expect at best for respect to be checked
because laying hands would be illegal
if I wrapped them around his neck
but that doesn't mean I'm gonna
let him run ravage with his demons
using anger that's been building up for years
to bully his peers because
the muscle between his ears
can't effectively connect with his heart,
and why are they now looking for a quick solution
when there was opportunity since birth
figuring, I'm suppose to know what to do
because my skin is brown
I'm a man and experienced

supposedly, having walked in his shoes
believe me, we aren't all the same
the game changes and
what I did to survive
won't be the same that keeps junior above ground
out of jail or in good standing in society
and if he's not going to take the time
to get educated
then he better learn how to socially behave
cause in a few years
he's going to have to be way more clever
since cute don't compute forgiveness
his peers currently doing all types of shit
like rape, getting chased
and/or shooting somebody in the face
and the boy just turned eight
so wait, Black man that's creating future men,
before you pass me the ball
this be that one time I don't want it
I'd rather much be part of the team
even if it's on the bench,
because the last time that man approached a bench
he was facing 12 peers and a 3 to 10
in-between then
I'm asking what's going to be left of his seed
and this grown man is now hoping for me to be
what he should have been ages ago
-a father-
and in turn, I end up martyred
somehow being blamed
because of the poor choices by those that are jailed
that look like me,

I entertain it constantly
especially when certain people walk in the school
and see me, judgin'
but I'm not buggin' because I got a job to do
if nobody else will
and that's all because
I care.

Mentees

Somebody told me that mentees (**don't quit**)
mentees (**don't quit**)
so I asked a few and they told me that
we are (**focused**), we are (**focused**)
in which I became more curious
because this was real serious
and it appeared as if they had the whole world
in the palm of their hand
(**if we can't do it, no one can**)
I said do you know what stands up against you
there's people just waiting to get a hold of you
be it, drug dealers or gang bangers
they sit and wait to claim
at the lost and rarely found
but these guys never looked down at the ground
they were proud of what they accomplished
saying mentees (**don't quit**)
despite the outfit, the looks
and brushes with negativity
one guy said people can only affect me if I let'em
so when I wake up I get set to go get'em
since I'm a go getter that's ready to
get something better
and I figured these guys were clever
however, I told him that
I keep hearing how at school
him and his friends are where the trouble begins
in fact,

the type of stereo playing wasn't in surround sound
the stereotype that was found
was a sad song singing of young boys
saggin' and laughin'
while certain grades they weren't passin'
but before I could get to askin'
these mentees (**don't quit**)
said excuse me sir but we are (**focused**)
so despite what you heard
let me give you the word
we rock 3 stars like we on the guitar
and we make moves like Malcolm X
if we need to go that far
but we're far from causing violence
when we have need to be at peace
so when you catch us in the hallway
we make a point to stop and speak
and we greet you with respect because
we've learned better
so no matter the weather
whenever there is greatness
we make it our forever
passion, to complete the task
and let the negativity pass
because the only thing stopping us from our destiny
is us if you ask
so if we laugh, please excuse us
but the hate we have to trash
and as the last sentence exited their mouths
I understood more what they were about
because mentees (**don't quit**), mentees (**don't quit**)
and when asked what they are they said

we are (**focused**), we are (**focused**)
so I took notice and felt good about
the future in front of me
knowing these guys had the whole world
in the palm of their hands
(**if we can't do it, no one can**)
I said they have the whole world
in the palm of their hands
(**if we can't do it, no one can**).

Period 4

She Spoke With Her Heart
(for the daughter that chose me)

It never entered my mind
that I would be here
right now,
you choosing me many moons ago
and I didn't truly accept it
til this moment,
it taking my heart being shattered into pieces
to hear what you spoke with yours
holding the opportunity
with the last bit of my shame
instructing you not to cry
as I knew it would cause me to
in front of others
-Thank You-
as even though you made the best attempts
to follow my direction
holding your hands to your face
in efforts to mask an expression so beautiful
I repeatedly asked God to forgive me
after refocusing on you from a distraction
in which, you let your happiness roll down cheeks
in liquid drops I should have caught
with my essence,
seeing now with your eyes
that never left from my position
currently piercing my existence

as only a daughter could do her father
not with malice but with the happiness
of witnessing the gift of love
being opened before them
yet, still unexpected in this way
and, that's ok
because you spoke with your heart
and rejoiced when I answered
with mine.

If She Knew, Then What

(for the daughter that chose me)

What if I told you
I love you so much
that I can't explain it
and I'm
struggling to contain it
and I'm
trying to explain it
in this poem.

What if I told you
I wanted,
no needed to be
that dad you chose me to be
finding perfect harmony
in the task of being
whatever it is the Universe is asking
through you.

What if I told you
I find you in my thoughts
continuously
subconsciously peeking through to
reality
running through my mind like
you belong here
and,
I'm believing that
you do.

What if I told you
you're becoming even more beautiful
with each memory
notched into history
complicated yet simply,
as I'm listening to you.

What if I told you
I'm going to be there
supporting what you do
without asking
or even when you do
cause, God keeps telling me
that's what I'm supposed to do.

What if I told you
the thought of losing you
hurts
-even if it's make believe-
and I send meditations
to the Universe
that you'd never grow tired
and leave.

What if I told you
you are powerful
beyond what you think
and you hold the key
with a team behind you
that's determined to help
you unlock dreams
into possibilities.

What if you knew
these things, I wonder
what if you knew
these things?

Let Me Ask Her

(for the daughter that chose me)

On the regular
I have questions
because fathers need daughters
to learn a few lessons
no need for second guessin
so right from the start
I'll begin by asking you
what's being held inside your heart
because it was crafted by God
a heavenly work of art
so make sure you protect it
because many would break it apart
and I know you're really smart
as it comes so easily
I often wonder within your mind
what's your fondest memory
seriously, can you tell me what makes you happy
or, why did that make you cry
here, come lean on my shoulder
as tears fall from your eyes
help me realize
what it is that makes you afraid
because whenever it is you need me
I'm beside you on center stage
I'll be that mage if you need magic
that's just one thing that I'd do
now tell me, what sort of things
are really important to you

what happened in your day
and, how did it make you feel
no need to keep it to yourself
let that stress go, for real
I'm for real, cause surely you just don't know
how important you are to me
what would you do, if this I showed
I sow these positive vibes into you
so, would that make you sing
I hope what this brings is happiness
from my core into your being
I'm wondering if, these words I speak
do they make you smile
cause I'm sitting in your energy
and I might be here for a while
so while, I'm in that memory
tell me what is you dream about
if you could do anything you wanted
how'd you make that dream turn out
let me help eliminate all doubt
if you ask, then I'll give more
for now I have to keep asking questions
like what kind of things make you feel cared for
and what do you need from me
or, what are the things that make you angry
how can I help alleviate negativity
and, what's been on your mind lately
cause lately, I've appreciated
what The Universe blessed me to be
"full heartedly" she calls me daddy
the letter "I" skipped over
meant I could be next to U, you see

so, do you understand what it is I'm saying
do you believe all these things to be true
and, if I could ask you only one more thing
do you know how much I love you?

Dorothy still Counts

James Baldwin said
we should have been there for Dorothy
to help our 15 year old daughter endure
the reality that sat on her shoulders
from integrating schools
and somehow
sixty four years later
as I teach students of all races
and
instead of a crowd of hate
the Universe opened the opportunity
for a student of a different ethnicity
to choose me
as her second dad
and I have the option
to choose
and accept that
which lets me know
"Dot" did more
than just integrate
a school system.

ISS

Teaching During Covid-19

Covid-19 left me wondering
what's worth more,
being authentically me
living the dream to educate
or debate sitting in place
so I wouldn't catch a case
spread a deadly fate
to those I relate to
risk my life just for the sake of
learning, the world is burning with
split decisions that's sending
people on a race against "human"
skin color does not relate
to the hate that's being injected with fear
and I hear, I'm labeled essential now
gear up against an enemy playing guerrilla warfare
and I'm aware of what's needed
that a vaccine or quarantine can't guarantee
put simply, choice is a matter of control
and the only thing I have that totally over is me,
so while the rush is on for some
to have teachers on the frontline
I'll remind those that the bigger picture
is not what it's made to seem
guess when focus is on selfish things
my life is deemed worth sacrificing,
for Covid-19

Homeroom

School Dad

The title "School Dad"
is not fit for every male educator
that enters into the school system,
it's a responsibility that is filled with love
and all to often
heartbreak
it's the wonder why you're awake
at God knows what hour
thinking about the well being
of a kid that's not even your own,
it's the 20 plus hours of preparation
for a moment
that physically last 2 minutes
but
means a lifetime in
the look, the smile
the thankless desire pushing tomorrow
for a butterfly that you feel flies away too soon,
you don't choose to be this guy
they choose you
for a moment
or a lifetime
whatever the reasons
it's them needing you
and then you realizing
you needed them
to heal, to learn
to remember that life doesn't deal coincidences
you either meet fate or fulfill destiny,

whichever is selected
they both echo into eternity
shaping the life of a young one
that has decided
-you're it-

"WE'RE ALL IN THIS TOGETHER"
- High School Musical
Thank you for everything you have taught
Me throughout these past 2 years, w/z more
to go. Before meeting you I never understood
what people meant when they say : i have
a second dad" or "i have a school dad" but
now I can full heartedly say that you are
my second dad. Thank you for everything
you have taught me and all the
stories we have shared and the laughs.
I LOVE YOU so, so MUCH!

About The Author

Billy Williams, Jr. was born to write poetry. Poetically knows as B-Dot and OnePoeticGamer, the life as a poet all started because of a girl back in 7th grade. Seeing he had a gift with words, he began to use his energy to produce poetry that spoke to various genres.

Hailing from Raleigh, North Carolina, Billy is a poet, educator, coach, gamer, streamer and motivator. School Dad is Billy's fourth book of published poetry, with more poetry books to be released in the near future.

If you want to find out more information about Billy's upcoming books, you can contact him by way of e-mail at onepoeticgamer@amazulugaming.com or sending a message to him from the following website www.amazulugaming.com. If you wish to know more about his gaming/streaming life, check him at www.twitch.tv/onepoeticgamer.

Social Media Contacts

Poetry Blog: www.amazulugaming.com
Instagram: Onepoeticgamer
Twitch: www.twitch.tv/onepoeticgamer

AmaZulu Gaming, LLC

Poetry Books Written By One Poetic

Poetic Superhero

Everybody is looking for a hero. Poetic Superhero is here for you.

The I prElude I

In order to find we, HE must find himself before finding SHE.

His Emotions Released

This is written for Her…I'm glad I finally got Her attention.

School Dad

Poetry inspired by 16 years of working as an educator in elementary, middle and high school.

the Book of HER (coming summer 2021)

33 poems for HER

Poetic Flows - A Book of Rhymes (upcoming 2021)

When I feel the flow, I let go with words.

<u>Spoken Word By One Poetic</u>

AM to PM - Audio Movement through Poetic Moves – an audio book (upcoming soon)

Spoken word that covers poems from Poetic Superhero, School Dad and His Emotions Released.

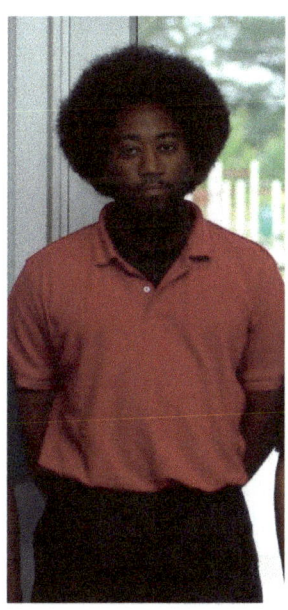